Leah Blackwell
Illustrations by Air Soft Studios

Grandma's Superstar

Bumblebee Books
London

A CIP catalogue record for this title is
available from the British Library.

ISBN: 978-1-83934-438-1

Bumblebee Books is an imprint of
Olympia Publishers.

First Published in 2021

Bumblebee Books
Tallis House
2 Tallis Street
London
EC4Y 0AB

Printed in Great Britain

www.olympiapublishers.com

Dedication

I would like to dedicate this book to all those families who are currently
visiting loved ones living well with dementia.

Grandma can't remember my name so she calls me her little superstar.

When we visit Grandma, she lives with lots of her friends in a big home and they also sometimes forget things. I do lots to cheer her up and to help her to remember the good times.

We bring her flowers to brighten the room and to help her remember that she was a florist. She helps me to arrange them in the vase and always puts her favourite colour at the front. (Can you see what Grandmas favourite colour is?)

She takes a step back to look at them and says, "What a superstar you are!"

I bring my story books from school and read them to Grandma and some of her friends.

I show them the pictures and make sure that I read nice and slowly so everyone can hear me. Once I've finished they all say, "What a superstar you are!"

If it's nice and sunny my mum helps Grandma with her walking frame into the garden and I carefully carry a tray of biscuits out to snack on because Grandma says you can't do anything on an empty stomach.

We bring some little plant pots onto the table outside and Grandma shows me how to put the soil in and how to plant the seeds. When I'm done and I show Grandma my finished pots she beams, "What a superstar you are!"

Once we get back inside Grandma does a big yawn, so my mum helps her to have a lay down on her bed for a little nap.

So I find a quiet corner to do my homework and colouring. Mum brings me over a drink and whispers, "What a superstar you are."

Grandma rings her bell when she's awake and it's just in time for tea! Grandma sits next to her friends and I pull up a chair next to them.

She has a delicious plate of fish and chips, but Grandma can't always remember what is on her plate and forgot what the green mushy things are. Do you know?

I reminded Grandma that they are called peas and she says, "Oh yes. What a superstar you are!"

After tea we usually relax in Grandmas room and I put on her favourite music and we get up and have a little dance. She says that it reminds her of when her husband took her dancing.

She started to get upset thinking about Grandad and asked where he was so I found the photo album in her bedside drawer and we had a look through together and this made Grandma smile as she says, "What a superstar you are!"

I don't like having to leave but I give Grandma a big hug and she's says I'll see you tomorrow which makes me smile.

I wave to all her friends on the way out and the carer gives me a high five as we leave and she says, "Thank you for being such a little superstar, you make your grandma very happy."

About the Author

Leah Blackwell is a first time author born in Salisbury, England. She has worked in dementia care for over seven years while achieving up to the level five management in health and social care. During this time Leah has experienced many children coming into the homes. The aim of this book is to help children to feel comfortable in care homes and to help parents to find a way of explaining the changes in their loved ones in a child friendly and positive way.

Printed in Great Britain
by Amazon